D1445795

Kylie Jean

Robot Queen

by Marci Peschke

illustrated by Tuesday Mourning

PICTURE WINDOW BOOKS
a capstone imprint

Kylie Jean is published by Picture Window Books
A Capstone Imprint
1710 Roe Crest Drive
North Mankato, Minnesota 56003
www.mycapstone.com

Library of Congress Cataloging-in-Publication Data
Cataloging-in-Publication information is on file with the Library of Congress.
Names: Peschke, Marci, author. | Mourning, Tuesday, illustrator.
Title: Robot Queen
ISBN 978-1-5158-2926-3 (library binding)
ISBN 978-1-5158-2934-8 (paper over board)
ISBN 978-1-5158-2930-0 (eBook PDF)

Creative Director: Nathan Gassman
Graphic Designer: Sarah Bennett
Editor: Shelly Lyons
Production Specialist: Kris Wilfahrt

Design Elements: Shutterstock

Printed and bound in Canada.
PA020

For:
My Guys
Jason, Wes, and Justin
— MP

Table of Contents

All About Me, Kylie Jean!

My name is Kylie Jean Carter. I live in a
big, sunny, yellow house on Peachtree Lane in
Jacksonville, Texas, with Momma, Daddy, and my
two brothers, T.J. and Ugly Brother.

T.J. is my older brother, and Ugly Brother is . . .
well . . . he's really a dog. Don't you go telling him
he is a dog. Okay? I mean it. He thinks he is a real
true person.

He is a black-and-white bulldog. His front looks
like his back, all smashed in. His face is all droopy
like he's sad, but he's not.

His two front teeth stick out, and his tongue hangs down. (Now you know why his name is Ugly Brother.)

Everyone I love to the moon and back lives in Jacksonville. Nanny, Pa, Granny, Pappy, my aunts, my uncles, and my cousins all live here. I'm extra lucky, because I can see all of them any time I want to!

My momma says I'm pretty. She says I have eyes as blue as the summer sky and a smile as sweet as an angel. (Momma says pretty is as pretty does. That means being nice to the old folks, taking care of little animals, and respecting my momma and daddy.)

But I'm pretty on the outside and on the inside. My hair is long, brown, and curly.

I wear it in a ponytail sometimes, but my absolute most favorite is when Momma pulls it back in a princess style on special days.

I just gave you a little hint about my big dream. Ever since I was a bitty baby I have wanted to be an honest-to-goodness beauty queen. I even know the wave. It's side to side, nice and slow, with a dazzling smile. I practice all the time, because everybody knows beauty queens need to have a perfect wave.

I'm Kylie Jean, and I'm going to be a beauty queen. Just you wait and see!

Chapter One
Code Day is Cool!

Slowly, I open one eye. My nose is chilly. It's a little cold in my room. I hear my alarm going off and Ugly Brother snoring. Suddenly, I realize it's Friday!

"Wake up, sleepyhead!" I shout.

I jump out of bed and pull on my jeans and shirt. I can't wait to go to school! Today is a special computer day at school called The Day of Code.

Ugly Brother is not excited about computers, but he follows me downstairs for breakfast. He is always excited about food!

When we get to the kitchen, Momma says, "You're up and dressed early today."

"Yes, ma'am," I reply. "Today is The Day of Code."

"What is that?" Momma asks.

"They have it every year in December," I tell her. "Last year we weren't able to do anything for it, but this year our teacher has big plans. The whole class is going to see and do some cool stuff on the computer. Code is computer language."

Momma says, "I knew that! Sounds like fun."

I eat my cinnamon toast in four gigantic bites and wash it down with a big glass of milk.

Momma frowns and asks, "Are you forgetting your manners, young lady?"

I shrug my shoulders. "Sorry, Momma," I say. "I'm just so excited!" I put on my pink coat and peek out the window. My breath makes the cold pane frosty.

Soon I hear the rumble of the bus as it rolls down the street. Momma also hears it and comes to the hall to kiss me goodbye. I dash down the sidewalk and scramble up the bus steps. My usual spot is next to my best cousin, Lucy, in the first row of seats. I find it and sit down.

Our bus driver, Mr. Jim, asks, "What's the rush, little lady?"

I smile and ask, "Do you like computers?"

"Sure do," he replies.

"Then you'd love The Day of Code!" I explain. "We get to do cool computer stuff all day today. I promise I'll tell you all about it this afternoon on my way home."

"Alrighty, then," he says. "I'd love to hear more about the coding day."

Lucy is excited too. She promises to help me remember everything so we can tell Mr. Jim.

Once at school, we head inside and go straight to class. After we hang up our coats in our cubbies, we sit down and wait for the day to begin. Ms. Corazon reminds us all about the assembly behavior rules and tells us to line up.

Lucy, Paula, Cara, and I line up together. The assembly is in the gym. Each class takes a seat on the bleachers.

Ms. Corazon calls, "Stick together, class!"

I am so excited, I sit right in the front row. Lucy, Paula, and Cara follow me.

Mr. Johnson, our principal, introduces The Day of Code. "This is a day that encourages everyone to code," he announces. "Today there will be no regular classes."

Everyone cheers! The kids go wild!

He continues, "You will be working on coding, computers, and projects all day, but first we have an exciting demonstration for you."

Suddenly from opposite sides of the gym, two robots zoom toward Mr. Johnson. One is pink, and the other is black and red. They stop and spin in circles beside the principal.

Mr. Johnson says, "These are robots from our school's robotics teams. Come on out, Ninjabots and RoboGirls!"

Several kids run out and stand in the middle of the gym, waving at us. Then the robots do another spin. Everyone in the gym claps like crazy!

The RoboGirls have pink shirts with their team name on them. I love them! Pink is my favorite color. I see a tall girl running the pink robot with something that looks like a video game controller. I also notice the RoboGirls are all girls. The other team, the Ninjabots, has both boys and girls.

They are wearing black and red shirts that say Ninjabots. A boy has their controller. He must be the team leader.

Mr. Johnson says, "Okay, robots, do your thing!"

The lights go dark and a spotlight shines on each robot. Music begins to play. Kids cheer and the robots begin to move around in a sort of dance.

Mr. Johnson says, "Ready . . . set . . . go!"

The robots race across the gym. At first the black and red robot is in the lead, but then the pink robot pulls ahead.

Mr. Johnson says, "Play nice."

The robots stop, and the two teams shake
hands with each other. Then the lights come back
on. The kids go crazy while the robots do another
spin.

Mr. Johnson says, "These exciting robots will be visiting classes all day."

The kids line up to leave the gym, but it's pretty chaotic. Some kids are getting in line with the wrong teachers.

I lean over and tell Lucy, "I sure hope the RoboGirls come to our class."

She says, "You just like their pink shirts."

I say, "Yup, and their pink robot too!"

Back in the classroom, Ms. Corazon has set up several different stations for us. Kids can either play computer games on the classroom computers, build with building blocks, or use the Fast Track game to code a car race using paper coding blocks and paper that shows the track. I try them all.

Right after lunch, the RoboGirls and their pink robot come to visit! The girls answer questions and tell us all about robotics competitions.

"Did you build the robot all by yourselves, without help from an adult?" I ask them.

"Of course!" they reply. "It's super fun and challenging too!"

Then they make the robot do tricks. We all clap and cheer.

That afternoon, on the way home, I tell Mr. Jim all about The Day of Code. Lucy helps me remember everything.

"I wish I could be on the robotics team," I tell Mr. Jim.

Chapter Two
FUNbot Fun

On Monday, the bus is buzzing with robot talk,
and at school, the halls are louder than usual.
If you think it's because kids are talking about
robots, you're right! All anyone can talk about
is robots, including me! I have decided to join a
robotics team. I can hardly wait until lunch to tell
my best cousin, Lucy, and my friends.

We find our favorite table and sit down. Before I even open my pink sparkly lunch box, I start talking. "I have BIG news!" I tell my friends.

Lucy says, "You didn't tell Mr. Jim or me on the bus this morning."

"I wanted to tell you all at once, and lunch is the perfect time," I reply. "I'm going to join one of the robotics teams!"

Paula asks, "Did you forget they are for older kids?"

"No, I didn't forget," I tell her. "I'm in second grade. They let in kids in grades three through five. Second grade is close to third grade. I'm hoping I can impress them so they'll ask me to join their club."

Lucy grins and suggests, "Make your own robot, and they might let you in!"

"That's a great idea," Cara chimes in.

Paula asks, "Do you know how to make one by yourself?"

"No," I reply, "but I saw some older kids make an art robot at the YMCA summer camp. It was cool, and I think I have everything I need to make one at home."

We all agree I have an awesome plan. I can hardly wait to get home and get started.

After school, I go on the computer and look up the directions for the robot I told everyone about. Ugly Brother watches me curiously. The directions look a little complicated, so I decide to check out some others.

When Ugly Brother sees an even better FUNbot made with little plastic blocks, he goes crazy.

"Do you think I can make this one?" I ask him.

"Ruff, ruff!" He replies. Two barks means yes.

He's pretty convinced I can do it. I will need to borrow some of T.J.'s old blocks, but he's not home yet. I know where he keeps them, though, so Ugly Brother and I head upstairs.

"Hopefully he won't mind if I borrow just a few blocks," I whisper. "I've got to get started if I'm going to build a robot tonight."

"Ruff, ruff!" Ugly Brother barks softly.

I open the door and head over to the closet on the back wall. Just then, I step on a block!

"Oopsie daisy!" I say.

Stepping over the block, I open the closet doors. In the back corner is a large tub of blocks. I pull it out into the room to sift through.

Just then, T.J. comes in and finds me digging in his tub. "Hey, what are you doing in here?" he asks.

"Just lookin' for some blocks," I tell him. "Can I please borrow some?"

"What for?" he asks.

"I'm building a robot for school," I explain.

"Well, you'll need more than blocks for that, but I guess you can use them if you're careful with them, okay?"

"Is putting duct tape on them going to mess them up?" I ask.

Frowning, he says, "Yes!"

"Never mind," I say as I put the bin back into the closet. "Come on, Ugly Brother!"

"What are you going to do?" T.J. asks.

"I have a plan B," I reply.

T.J. nods his head and puts his headphones on as Ugly Brother and I walk out of the room.

"It's a good thing I have a plan B," I tell Ugly Brother.

"Ruff, ruff!" he replies.

The two of us decide to do some research. On my tablet, we look up different kinds of robots. We find one that can be made with a pool noodle. We have a pool noodle in our garage. I will also need duct tape, markers, scissors, paper, and a battery-operated toothbrush.

Ugly Brother and I head out to the garage and grab the pool noodle and duct tape. As we're going through the kitchen, I stop and look at Momma, who is sitting at the table with a book.

"May I use my toothbrush for a school project?" I ask her.

"Your toothbrush?" she asks.

"Yes, I want to build a robot for the robotics team," I explain.

"I suppose you can use your toothbrush. There's an extra one in the closet," she says. "It sounds like a fun project! Can I help?"

"Sure can!" I reply. "I need a grown-up to cut the pool noodle about the length of my toothbrush."

Momma gets out her electric kitchen knife and cutting board. She zips right through the pool noodle. Then I put the toothbrush inside the pool noodle's center hole.

Next, we tape the markers on the outside edge of the noodle evenly with the marker points down.

Momma says, "I see you are using pink, purple, and red markers."

"Yup!" I say. "You know pink is my best color!"

Momma brings out some hot pink yarn for hair and some googly eyes to add to the lime green pool noodle. My FUNbot is finished! Now we just need to turn it on and make sure it works.

Momma gets a piece of paper. I take the lids off the markers and set the robot on the paper on the kitchen table. Then I turn on the toothbrush. It's working!

"Hooray! Yay! Yipeee!" Momma and I cheer.

Momma says, "Let's give it a name."

"Great idea!" I say. "How about Fluffy? It does have fluffy yarn hair."

"Love it!" replies Momma.

Ugly Brother runs around barking at the buzzing of the robot.

"Calm down, Ugly Brother," I tell him. "It's just my robot, Fluffy."

Turning it off, I show it to him. Then I show him the picture my FUNbot just made all by itself! I can't wait to take it to school and see if my plan works. If the big kids like it, maybe I can be a robot queen!

Chapter Three
Code Chimp

On Tuesday, I wake up when the rooster crows because today is a big day! I carefully pack my FUNbot to take it to school. I pack Fluffy in a shoebox with balls of paper along the sides to keep my robot from rolling around in the box.

After breakfast, I brush my teeth with the new toothbrush Momma gave me yesterday. My old toothbrush has been transformed into my robot, Fluffy. Then I head back downstairs to get my backpack and watch for my bus.

Momma asks, "Where is Fluffy?"

"Don't worry, Momma!" I reply. "Fluffy is safe inside a shoebox in my backpack."

I point to my backpack. Then I hear the bus coming down the street. I give Momma some "sugar," and she gives me a kiss too.

After I get settled on the bus, I share my news with Lucy and Mr. Jim. "You won't believe it, but I've got a brand new robot in my backpack," I tell them.

Mr. Jim says, "Wow!"

"I made it at home," I continue, "and Momma only had to help a teensy, tiny bit."

"I'm impressed," he says.

"Awesome!" Lucy says as she gives me a high-five. "I knew you could do it!"

All I have to do now is impress the robotics team kids. I take Fluffy with me to lunch. I'm so excited, I can hardly eat my sandwich. After I eat, I unpack the robot. I set Fluffy up on some paper and start my robot.

Cara looks over and says, "You're going to get in that club now. You built a robot!"

Paula says, "Yeah, your plan is going to work. I just know it."

Other kids start gathering around to watch Fluffy, including one of the RoboGirls girls.

This is it! I think to myself. Now I'm going to be invited to join the club!

But the RoboGirl girl doesn't look impressed. "That's a cute FUNbot," she says. "If you like tinkering with technology, you should try Code Chimp."

I am so sad as she walks away. She only thinks my robot is cute. But I'm not giving up, and now I'm going to find a way to try Code Chimp.

Lucy suggests, "Maybe your momma will buy it for you. Then you can try to get in the club again."

Paula says, "You can say it's part two of your plan."

It seems like school will never end! I need to get home and ask Momma if we can buy Code Chimp. When I finally get home, I race off the bus and into the kitchen.

Momma asks, "What's the rush?"

I blurt out, "Can we get Code Chimp?"

Momma asks, "Are you saying that you want to buy a computer monkey?"

I explain, "It's not actually a chimp. A girl at school told me about it. It's a tiny credit card-sized computer that you can attach to a monitor and a keyboard. The best part is that it's so easy to program, a chimp could do it!"

Momma's eyes get big. I can tell she is surprised! "Where do you get this tiny computer board?" she asks. "Do we order it online? Is it expensive?"

"We can order it on the Internet," I tell her. "But I don't know how much they cost."

Moments later we are on the computer looking at a website. Momma whistles. "It's an expensive toy, and I can't believe a chimp can code this. It looks complicated."

"Well, it's not really a toy," I explain. "It's a tiny computer."

We decide to compromise. I have most of the money saved up from allowances and a little birthday money. Momma says if I choose a less expensive kit, she'll help me with the rest. The company we are ordering from promises free shipping. I can hardly wait. It seems like it will take a long, long, long time for my kit to arrive.

"I think you need to find something to help you pass the time," Momma suggests. "Let's have an afternoon snack, and Fluffy can entertain us."

"Okie dokie," I reply.

Momma gets out cheese and crackers. It's my favorite after-school snack. We eat, chat, and watch Fluffy spin around and around making cool, colorful circles on the paper in the middle of the table.

I decide to spend the rest of the afternoon and after dinner online reading about Code Chimp. Ugly Brother keeps me company at my feet. I learn a lot, but I still have some questions. Before I go to bed, I make a list of things I don't understand. I need answers.

T.J. walks over and taps me on the shoulder. "Time for bed, Lil' Bit," he says.

"Have you heard of Code Chimp?" I ask him.

"Yeah, my friend Randall had one," he says.

"I'm getting one with my allowance money," I tell him.

"Cool!" he says. "What are you going to do with it?"

"Build a robot!" I reply.

"Wow! Code Chimp is a great place to start. But it might be a little hard for a little kid to build a robot without help," he explains. "You could call my friend. I'll give you his number, and he can answer your questions."

"Thanks, T.J.!" I say as I jump up and give him a hug. "I've made up my mind to build a real true robot! Just you wait and see."

Ugly Brother is listening, and he barks twice as if to say, "Yes, you can!"

Chapter Four
Makerspace

On Wednesday, my special package has STILL not arrived! I just want it to get here so I can get started on my robot. I complain to Ugly Brother.

Momma says, "Be patient. Good things come to those who wait. Besides, we can't complain because we got free shipping!"

"Yes, ma'am," I say.

I'm still anxious for my package to arrive. Finally, my special order arrives on Friday.

After school, Momma is waiting at the door. "Guess who got a package in the mail today?" she asks.

"Me! Me!" I shout.

I hand Momma my backpack and lunch box. Then I tear into my package. Inside is everything I will need to power my robot. Reading the instructions is my first job, so I head right for my room.

Momma asks, "What about your afternoon snack?"

"No, thank you, Momma," I reply. "I've got a lot to get done if I'm going to build another robot this weekend."

***

After reading all about Code Chimp for the last two days, I know I will have to build my actual robot before I can program it. This could be a real problem.

Ugly Brother jumps up on the chair.

I say, "I'm not sure I have the supplies to make a robot."

He tilts his head and looks at me like he doesn't understand. I'm so close to figuring this out, but I need help.

I ask, "Where can we get help?"

Ugly Brother just rolls over.

"That's not very helpful," I say. "But we'll see if we can think of anything tomorrow morning."

When I wake up the next day, Ugly Brother is sitting at my bedroom door. I think he needs to go outside, so we head downstairs. But he won't go out!

"Do you want me to go out too?" I ask.

"Ruff, ruff!" he barks.

"Okay, I'll just run up and get dressed," I reply.

When I get back downstairs, I realize Ugly Brother wants to go for a walk. I grab his leash and connect it to his collar. When I step onto the porch, I see Daddy sitting in his chair, drinking coffee.

"We're going for a walk," I tell him.

"Okay if I tag along?" Daddy asks as he walks toward us.

"Yes, sir!" I reply.

Ugly Brother barks, "Ruff, ruff."

We chat all the way down Peachtree Lane. When we get to the end of our street, Ugly Brother wants to keep on going, so we do — all the way to the town square.

"We sure are getting our exercise in!" Daddy exclaims.

When we turn around to head back home, Ugly Brother sits down on the sidewalk, right in front of the Jacksonville Library.

Daddy looks down at him and says, "I think he wants a book."

I laugh and remind Daddy that Ugly Brother can't actually read. Then I look at the door and see a giant poster that says, Makerspace Saturdays: Come and Make Something. And I do need to make something! I don't know if this is an accident or if somehow my doggie brother knew how to help me, but I am so glad. I bend down and give him a quick hug.

"Daddy, can we please go in?" I ask.

He says, "We haven't had breakfast yet, and we don't want to leave Ugly Brother out here. I'll bring you back later today. I promise."

I agree, so we hurry home, eat breakfast, and hurry back. The library is full of people! It must be because of the new makerspace. They have turned the large event room into a creation station. Daddy is impressed too. He goes to look at a special saw.

A lady is making something pink in a clear box with plastic.

"What is it?" I ask her.

She says, "This is a 3D printer, and I'm making a soap dish."

"Pink is my favorite color," I tell her. "I love your dish!"

The lady nods and keeps watching the printer. I see a table topped with colorful plastic robot parts, and lots of kids are crowded around it. They are all building things, so I head over.

The librarian, Ms. Patrick, stops me. "Are you just playing, or will you want to keep what you make?" she asks.

"I'm making a robot, and I'll want to keep it," I tell her.

"You'll need to sign in and pay a small fee at the desk over there," she explains.

"Yes, ma'am," I reply.

I go get Daddy. He pays for me to build my robot. Then I tell him I don't need any more help, so he goes back to watching the men using the big, fancy saw.

Back at the table, I get busy. Before long, I've created a square robot on wheels. It's made out of small plastic parts and is about the size of a pasta bowl. The robot is kind of plain and needs a little razzle-dazzle. When I get home, I'll have to fix it up.

Ms. Patrick says, "That's innovative. Do you know how to program your robot?"

"Yes, ma'am," I reply. "I'm going to use Code Chimp."

She says, "That's a great tool for a beginner. Your robot is going to be awesome! Maybe we could display it when you are done. Other kids could see what cool things you can make in our new makerspace."

"Thanks," I say. "This robot has a job to do first, but when we're done, I'll bring it back to visit you."

Ms. Patrick smiles at me just as Daddy comes over to see if I'm ready to go yet. I'm ready!

Back at home, I go straight to my room where Ugly Brother is waiting. I give him a big squeezy hug and show him the robot.

"We have to jazz it up," I tell him.

He agrees. I give my robot googly eyes with big eyelashes made of craft fringe, then I spray it with silver glitter. I love it!

Next, I start to program it. Code Chimp is supposed to be easy to use. It is a lot like a microcontroller board. We learned about control boards at school. I can drag and drop to create my program, so I create a program to make it move forward. Then I test it. The robot rolls forward and Ugly Brother barks and chases it.

I say, "No, no, you can't play with the robot, but maybe you can help name it."

"Do you like the name Star?" I ask him.

"Ruff!" he replies. One ruff means no.

"How about Eyebot?" I ask.

Again, one bark. He does not like that name either. But then I finally think of the perfect name!

"Glitterbot?" I ask.

Ugly Brother goes wild, barking and running around. He loves it!

"I think she wants to dance," I say. "Let's program her to spin."

A short while later, I test the newest part of my program, and Glitterbot spins on my bedroom floor.

"Cool!" I say. "I'm ready to impress the big kids!"

Now I will have to wait all day Sunday, but on Monday we'll see if my robot can help me get on a robotics team.

Chapter Five
Battlebots

I am super excited on Monday morning,
because I am finally taking my Glitterbot to
school! When I get on the bus, I sit right behind
Mr. Jim so I can show it to him. It's a short drive
to school, but I'll have to wait until we get there
because Mr. Jim is busy driving the bus now.
Lucy and I talk the whole way. I tell her all
about making my robot. She wants to visit the
makerspace at the library and make a soap dish
with the 3D printer.

We pull up in front of the school. As soon as all the other kids get off the bus, I open my box so Mr. Jim can see my robot.

Mr. Jim says, "I'm eager to see that robot in action."

"Her name is Glitterbot, and she's got moves!" I tell him.

I can't be late for school, so I quickly set my robot down and use my controller to roll her down the bus aisle.

Mr. Jim shouts, "Fantastic!"

"Watch this!" I cry.

I press more buttons and Glitterbot spins. Mr. Jim gasps. "Now I've seen it all," he says. "A robot on my bus! You're a genius, little lady."

Smiling, I say, "Thank you very much. It's my secret dream to be on a robotics team!"

He winks and says, "Well, I wish you the best of luck. I hope your plan works."

"Me too!" I exclaim.

In the classroom, I let my best cousin, Lucy, and my friends peek inside the box.

Lucy squeals, "That robot is so you! How did you get the glitter to stay on it?"

"Easy," I explain. "I used spray glue, and it worked perfectly. I can't wait to show everyone what my Glitterbot can do at lunch!"

In class, it's hard to pay attention. I keep daydreaming about being on a robotics team. Time is inching by. I stare out the window and see a cloud that looks like a robot! In science, we are talking about energy.

I whisper to Lucy, "I want to talk about computer power instead."

Finally, lunchtime arrives. Ms. Corazon calls our class to line up. I carry my lunch box and my bot box. In the cafeteria, kids are rushing to get in line for food. I glance at the shiny steel lunch counter and see that the line is long today. It snakes along the wall all the way to the door. I pick a table right in the center of the room. I want us to be the center of attention so I can make sure everyone sees my Glitterbot.

Carefully, I remove it from the box and set it on the table. Then, while I nibble on my cheese sandwich, I use my controller to make my robot roll back and forth across the table. When I see a RoboGirl coming, I make Glitterbot spin in the middle of the table. She reminds me of a disco ball with all her silver glitter.

Maggie, the RoboGirl, stops right in the middle of the aisle, and two kids bump into her! Paula, Cara, and Lucy come around the other side and sit down. They are practically hypnotized by my Glitterbot. Now other kids are stopping to watch Glitterbot too!

Maggie asks, "Hey, where did you get that robot?"

I smile and say, "I made it."

"No way!" she replies.

"Yes, way!" I tell her. "I made it at the library's new makerspace, and I used Code Chimp to program it."

"Wow, your robot is super cool!" says Maggie. She calls over some of the other RoboGirls to see it.

"My robot's name is Glitterbot," I tell them.

One of them asks, "What grade are you in?"

"Second, but I really, really want to be on a robotics team!" I reply.

Just then, two Ninjabot kids come over.

The tall one is Clinton, the team captain. He watches my bot and asks some questions.

"If you're looking for a team, you can join us," he tells me. "You might be a second grader, but if you built that, you know robots!"

Maggie says, "I saw her first, Clinton! We want her to be a RoboGirl."

Lucy leans over and says, "Wow, the team leaders are acting like battlebots over you."

I am ready to jump for joy! Just then, Claire, the girl who told me about Code Chimp, walks up. "What's going on?" she asks.

The RoboGirls tell her about me, my Glitterbot, and the Ninjabots trying to steal me for their team.

Claire says, "I can settle this right now. I'm the one who told this girl about Code Chimp, and that means we RoboGirls knew this girl first."

Clinton asks me if it's true. I nod my head.

He says, "Too bad. I'd like you to be a Ninjabot, but I have to be fair."

Maggie and Claire start chanting, "RoboGirls! RoboGirls!"

Then Maggie says, "We'll see you at the next team meeting on Wednesday after school. Ms. Hopkins is our sponsor, and we meet in her lab."

I'm so excited and happy, I can't seem to say a thing, so I just nod my head again. Lucy and my friends jump up and down. I can't wait to tell everyone that I'm going to be a RoboGirl!

Later when I get home, I tell Momma and Ugly Brother. Momma is so happy for me, she gives me a big squeezy hug. Ugly Brother tries to jump up and get in on the hug too! Then she lets me pick what we're going to have for dinner to celebrate my big news. I choose spaghetti and meatballs. I can't wait to tell T.J. and Daddy. This has got to be one of my very best days ever!

Chapter Six
Mini RoboGirl

Today is club day! My very first day on the
robotics team as a real RoboGirl! Our club meets
in the STEAM lab. STEAM stands for Science,
Technology, Engineering, Art, and Math. Right
after school ends, I head straight for the lab.
The lab has long tables, computer stations,
engineering parts, tubs of colorful plastic robot
parts, and posters of robots on the walls. Inside I
see Claire and Maggie. I also see Ms. Hopkins, the
STEAM teacher.

Ms. Hopkins reaches out to shake my hand and says, "Welcome to the team."

I shake her hand. "Thanks, so much!" I reply.

Maggie says, "Hey, new girl. Ready to rumble with a robot battle?"

"Yup! How can I help?" I ask.

Claire says, "We have someone we want you to meet. Kylie Jean, meet Pinkerella the Destroyer, Pinkie for short."

"Pleased to meet you, Pinkie!" I say. "Pink is my favorite color."

Maggie, our team leader, explains that the RoboGirls and the Ninjabots will be competing in a regional robotics competition on Saturday.

"We will need all of our club members if we're going to win," she explains. "Claire is passing out permission slips. You must have your permission slip on Saturday to compete."

The team wants to practice with their robot. Claire explains to everyone that the challenges the robot must complete will be like a relay race. Ms. Hopkins gives her a list of the challenges:

CHALLENGES:

Robot Requirements:
Lifting and stacking cones
Moving forward
Moving backward
Spinning

Pinkie will be competing this time. The team has been working on programing her for the competition. First, we decide to conduct a quick test of our robot's ability to lift and stack the cones.

Maggie says, "I'll get the cones ready!"

Claire says, "Great. I'll set Pinkie up."

I sure hope the test goes well. I'm crossing my fingers!

"Okay, are we ready?" asks Claire.

Maggie nods her head. Claire takes the controller and starts Pinkie's test. The robot rolls smoothly over a white mat toward the cones and stops. We hold our breath as it picks up the first cone. Then we all sigh as it struggles to stack the cone on top of next cone.

"Bummer!" says Maggie. "I thought we might have trouble with our robot picking the cones up. I didn't think about stacking them."

"Hey, look at it this way," replies Claire. "We've already passed the first challenge. All we have to do is figure out the second."

Claire calls us all to one of the lab tables. We set Pinkie in the middle of the table.

"Okay, RoboGirls, we need to figure out what's going on with our stacking problem. Who has a solution?" asks Claire.

Everyone around the table starts to talk at the same time. Together we decide two things may be holding our robot back.

Maggie says, "I think we need to program Pinkie's arm so it can lift the cones higher."

Another girl thinks we need to make Pinkie's arm longer too. It would be an easy change.

Claire says, "Putting a longer arm on is easy, but if it's too long, it could get in the way."

"Could we build an arm that folds in and out?" I ask.

Maggie says, "Cool! You mean it could be long or short, right?"

"Yes," I reply.

"Let's divide the tasks," says Claire. "Maggie and Kylie Jean can work on building the new arm, and the rest of us will reprogram the arm."

We get right to work. There is a cabinet that has tubs of parts and robotics supplies. We head over to grab some parts.

"I think we need a hinge," I say as I open the cabinet.

"Yes, probably two for each arm, so they can fold out and in," says Maggie.

While we build the new arm, we listen to the girls who are working on the coding. They make a change and test it. It is still not enough, so they tweak the code some more.

When they are close, Claire asks if the new arm is ready. "I really think this two-part fix is going to work!" she tells us.

We watch while Claire uses the controller to guide Pinkie to pick up cones and stack them. We all cheer!

Pinkie follows the white path across the mat to return to us.

I ask, "Does the light sensor help the robot stay on the path?"

Claire says, "Yes! You sure do know a lot about robots."

"I've been doing some research on the Internet," I tell her.

"How did our robot get her name?" I ask.

Claire says, "We all like Cinderella, but we wanted a fierce robot. Since we wear pink T-shirts, we went with Pinkerella."

We run our robot backward and forward. Then we take her for a spin.

We want to beat the Ninjabots! Pinkie is ready! We are ready!

Just then, Claire says, "Kylie Jean is not ready."

I'm shocked! Everyone knows how hard I've been working. Then Ms. Hopkins hands me a bag. I stuff my hand into the bag and feel soft fabric.

Maggie asks, "Do you know what it is?"

"I'm guessing it's my shirt," I reply.

Pulling it out of the bag, I see a pink RoboGirls T-shirt.

"I love it, and I love pink!" I tell them.

Ms. Hopkins reminds everyone to arrive early on Saturday.

"Are any parents coming to watch us compete?" she asks.

"Yes, mine will be there," I say.

A few others on the team say yes as well. Claire calls us in to make a circle. She explains that the team always ends meetings with a circle.

"Ready, team?" Claire asks as we huddle up.

"YES!" we yell. "RoboGirls! RoboGirls!"

We are going to rock the competition. We are ready to compete!

Chapter Seven
Coding Competition

On Saturday, I wake up ready to robot rumble!
Our competition is just hours away. I put on my
jeans, pink sneakers, and my RoboGirls T-shirt.
Ugly Brother is so excited, he dances around while
I get dressed. It's going to break his little puppy
dog heart when I tell him he can't come with me
and meet Pinkie.

"Sorry, Ugly Brother," I tell him. "You'll have
to stay home. They don't let dogs come to the
competition."

He barks, "Ruff."

That means no, and he might not like it, but he can't come with us. I'm feeling sad. But suddenly I get a terrific idea!

"If you stay here, we can build a robot puppy together later. Would you like that?"

He barks, "Ruff, ruff."

Now he's happy and I am too. Building another robot will be fun!

We eat breakfast, and I do homework. When it's time to leave, Momma and Daddy call me. I'm not even nervous. We head to the community college for the competition.

"Are you ready?" asks Momma.

I say, "Yup, I have a great team!"

Daddy adds, "Win or lose, I'm proud of you, sugar. You really wanted to be the youngest member of the robotics team, and here you are going to your first competition!"

I say, "Thank you!"

Inside is a check-in table. Hanging all around the room are huge banners with the names of all the teams on them. When I see Claire, I wave. Momma and Daddy walk me over to the check-in table so I can sign in and get my official badge.

Claire points me to a to a big room filled with more tables. Teams are setting up everywhere, and the room is a sea of colorful T-shirts. Each has a team name printed on it. I see Go Go Gadgets, Princess Programmers, Terminators, TechieTreckers, and the Ninjabots.

The Ninjabots wave, and I wave back.

It's so exciting! I'm at a real true robotics competition. Suddenly, I feel butterflies tumbling around in my stomach. I might be getting a little nervous.

Claire calls our team together and explains that we need one more practice run. She says that sometimes glitches happen at the last minute.

Momma and Daddy go sit with the other parents. As they leave, Momma winks and gives me a thumbs-up. We put Pinkie on the course and get her ready to go.

Claire says, "Kylie Jean, this is your first official competition. I think you should have the controller."

My eyes flash with sheer happiness as I press the buttons on the controller and Pinkie starts to move. She rolls over to the path. So far everything is A-OK. Our team is cheering for Pinkie. But just before she starts stacking the cones, the arm fails!

Maggie says, "Uh-oh, we have a problem!"

"Team, we need to figure this out fast," Claire warns.

I don't want us to lose before we even start! I think and think some more. Sometimes when I am figuring out a problem, I think back to everything that has already happened. At our club meeting, everything was okay, or was it?

"I think I know what's wrong!" I shout.

Claire asks, "Can you fix the coding error, or do you need help?"

"I've got this!" I tell her. "It's a problem with the hinges."

I find the code block and adapt the code for opening the arm. We RoboGirls are ready to try again. This time Pinkie makes it to the first cone, picks it up, and stacks it on the second cone on the first try. My team goes wild cheering for me.

The room is getting louder and louder as teams get ready to compete. Soon the judges come by. They are asking if the team leader will be at the controls.

Claire pauses, then says, "I think we should let Kylie Jean run Pinkie for this first round. She is the newest member, and she saved the day with her smart coding."

The team shouts, "Yes!"

I get in position, and Claire places Pinkie in the playing field.

The team leader for the opposing team, the Princess Programmers, has their controller. One of her teammates puts their robot on the table in front of the starting line beside Pinkie.

The judge has a timer in his hand. He says, "Ready . . . set . . . go!"

I press the buttons on the controller, and the judge starts the timer. Pinkie moves quickly down the path to the cones. Now for the true test: can she stack them?

We all hold our breath. If she doesn't get it done on the first try, we could lose the competition.

Pinkie picks up the first cone and successfully puts it on top of the second cone. When she reaches the end of the path, she spins around and returns backward to the starting line in record time. We won! The Princess Programmers' robot started out fast, but has suddenly slowed down.

I say, "Hey, they must have a glitch too! Can I help them?"

"Yes, you'd be doing them a favor by being a good sport," replies Claire.

While the RoboGirls move to the next playing field to compete with the Terminators, who just won on their field, I stay behind to help the Princess Programmers. Their captain is a girl named Daisy, and their all-white robot is called Snow White.

Daisy asks, "Anyone have any ideas about speeding up our robot?"

"Can I try to help?" I ask.

Daisy says, "At this point, we'll take all the help we can get."

We talk about their program and how many rotations per minute they have coded for the wheels to spin. The team decides to change the number of rotations. After they make the change in their code, it's time to test the robot. I'm trying to watch their test and see my team competing at the same time. It looks like we are winning against the Terminators!

The new program is helping the Princesses' robot go a little faster, but it's still not speeding along. Suddenly, I have another idea!

"Can I pick up your robot?" I ask.

Daisy replies, "Sure."

I carefully lift Snow White. She is heavier than Pinkie! "I think your robot is a little heavy," I tell them.

Daisy says, "We were worried that she might be. For the next competition, we'll have to make some changes."

Meanwhile, my team is moving through the matches. There are eight matches total. For our final match we are going to compete with another team against two other teams. These are alliance competitions. All teams will compete with their robot, and we can earn points toward our final score. With the changes the Princesses made to Snow White, they have been racking up points. We are forming our alliance with them. Our competition will be our other school team, the Ninjabots, who are allied with the Terminators.

Claire takes the controller. She is ready! Pinkie is ready!

We cheer, "Go Claire, and come on Pinkie!"

Clinton and his robot are slightly behind Pinkie. I am watching Snow White, and she is faster than the Terminators' robot too.

Pinkie keeps the lead, and we win! My team goes crazy, jumping up and down, giving each other high-fives, and cheering.

The win gives our team even more points, pushing us into the lead for total points. The RoboGirls get the first-place trophy! It's huge, with a gold robot on top.

Daddy and Momma rush over and take our picture with the trophy.

It's a great day for the Ninjabots too. They came in second and get a smaller trophy with a little silver robot on top. The trophy case at school is going to be much fuller now. We robo-rocked our competition!

Chapter Eight
Puppy-Bot

After the competition, Momma, Daddy, and I head home. I'm so excited, I can't wait to tell Ugly Brother all about it. I have a promise to keep too. It takes us about ten minutes to get back to our house on Peachtree Lane. T.J. is outside mowing the grass.

As we get out of the van, he shouts, "How did it go, Lil' Bit?"

I run across the yard and tell him all about our big trophy. He gives me a high-five! As I walk up to the back door, I see Ugly Brother's face looking out at me. He has been waiting for me all morning. I open the door and step inside.

"I bet you want to know all about my competition, right?" I ask.

He barks, "Ruff, ruff."

"It was awesome!" I tell him. "We won, and I helped another team too. Now I'm going to make a puppy-bot."

He barks excitedly, "Ruff, ruff."

We go upstairs, and I get out the box with my Glitterbot inside. I also grab my craft box with all sorts of art supplies in it.

"We're going to make Glitterbot into a puppy!"
I tell him. Do you want to help me make the
puppy?"

"Ruff! Ruff!" he replies.

I twist tape around and around to make a thick
tail. I set it aside. Then I cut two long ears out of
construction paper. Next I carefully cut out some
black spots. I attach the ears and spots to the robot
with tape.

"What do you think?" I ask.

Ugly Brother barks, "Ruff, ruff."

I add a pink pom-pom for a nose. Now it's time
for the tail, but when I reach for it, it's not there!
I turn around and see Ugly Brother holding it in
his mouth like a bone.

"It's your turn to help," I tell him. "Bring me the tail, please."

He barks twice and drops it right beside the puppy-bot. I tape on the tail and grab my controller. The puppy-bot spins, and the puppy ears flap a little.

"What should we name this new robot?" I ask.

Ugly Brother looks at me but doesn't bark. He is out of ideas. I think and think.

"How about SpotBot?"

Ugly Brother barks and barks. I think he likes this new robot.

Daddy peeks in and asks, "Where did that robot come from?"

I reply, "It's a new old robot. I made GlitterBot
into SpotBot for Ugly Brother because he was
so sad that he couldn't come with us to the
competition this morning."

Daddy smiles and says, "You have a good heart, Kylie Jean. Helping that other team at the competition and building this robot for Ugly Brother makes me really proud of you!"

I grin and say, "Thanks, Daddy."

"Now, come downstairs," he says. "I made us some lunch, Robot Queen!"

Marci Bales Peschke was born in Indiana, grew up in Florida, and now lives in Texas with her husband, two children, and a cat named Cookie. She loves reading and watching movies.

When **Tuesday Mourning** was a little girl, she knew she wanted to be an artist when she grew up. Now, she is an illustrator who lives in Utah. She especially loves illustrating books for kids and teenagers. When she isn't illustrating, Tuesday loves spending time with her husband, who is an actor, and their two sons and one daughter.

Glossary

3D printer (THREE-DEE-PRIN-tur)—a machine that creates objects that are 3-dimensional

chaotic (kay-AH-tik)—a feeling of total confusion

compromise (KAHM-pruh-myz)—to reach an agreement

engineering (en-juh-NEER-ing)—using science to design and build things

hypnotize (HIP-nuh-tyz)—to put another person in a sleeplike state

impress (im-PRESS)—to make someone think highly of you

makerspace (MAY-kur SPAYS)—a space where people can create and tinker

relay race (REE-lay RAYSS)—a team racing event; each team usually has four members

rotation (roh-TAY-shuhn)—a circular motion made by a part or object

sponsor (SPON-sur)—someone responsible for a program

tinker (TING-kur)—to make small adjustments to something in a casual way

Talk!

1. Why do you think Daddy said he was proud of Kylie Jean for helping at the competition and for making the puppy bot? What's something you have done that made yourself or others proud?

2. Kylie Jean really wants to join a robotics team. Is there a team or club you'd like to join? How could you make that happen?

3. Kylie Jean says that when she's figuring out a problem, she thinks back to everything that has already happened. How do you like to figure out problems?

Be Creative!

1. Imagine you are going to design a robot. Draw a picture of what it might look like. Now, list three things it might do. Give your bot a creative name!

2. Write a letter to the RoboGirls or Ninjabots and explain why you should be a member of their team.

3. Kylie Jean joins the RoboGirl team. Imagine you are a member of the RoboGirls. Write and decorate a poster advertising your team to kids in school who want to join.

This recipe makes a fun group activity!

Love, Kylie Jean

From Momma's Kitchen

Robot Crispy Pops

YOU NEED:

- ¼ cup butter
- 4 cups mini marshmallows
- 5 cups crispy rice cereal
- Assorted candies for decoration. You will need something for the eyes and mouth. Try circular or square candies, or a mix!
- Icing in your favorite color
- Popsicle or lollipop sticks

1. Melt butter in large saucepan over low heat. Add marshmallows and stir until melted and well-blended. Cook a few minutes longer, stirring constantly. Remove from heat.

2. Add cereal. Stir until well coated.

3. Press mixture (with clean fingers!) evenly and firmly in a buttered 13 x 9 inch pan.

4. Cool in the fridge. Then cut into rectangles.

5. Carefully insert a lollipop (or Popsicle) stick into each rectangle.

6. Now, use the icing to "glue" on the candies to create your robot. Give it sensors, eyes, ears, and a mouth.

7. Give your robot a name and imagine all the things it can do . . . that is . . . until you eat it!

Yum!

THE FUN DOESN'T STOP HERE!

Discover more at www.capstonekids.com

♥ Videos & Contests
❀ Games & Puzzles
♥ Friends & Favorites
❀ Authors & Illustrators

Find cool websites and more books like this one at www.facthound.com. Just type in the Book ID: **9781515829263** and you're ready to go!